Wash-a-Bye BEAR

For Bethan, Lucia and Tilly

A TEMPLAR BOOK

First published in the UK in hardback in 2012 by Templar Publishing
This softback edition published in 2013 by Templar Publishing,
an imprint of The Templar Company Limited,
Deepdene Lodge, Deepdene Avenue, Dorking, Surrey, RH5 4AT, UK
www.templarco.co.uk

Copyright © 2012 by Thomas Docherty

www.thomasdocherty.co.uk

1 3 5 7 9 10 8 6 4 2

ISBN 978-1-84877-827-6

Printed in China

Thomas Docherty

Wash-a-Bye BEAR

templar publishing

"I love you, Bear," said Flora one morning.

"But Mummy says you are smelly and full of bits
and you need a wash."

"So you're going in
the washing machine with
all the dirty socks."

"Don't worry, Bear, I'm going to be right here
waiting for you."

"Be brave, Bear!"

Wash away soggy breakfast smears...

wash away melted ice cream tears.

Wash away memories of the beach...

birthday cake and sticky sweets.

Wash away spatters of winter showers…

wash away mud and rain-soaked hours.

Wash away scrapes from climbing trees...

hide-and-seek in autumn leaves.

Wash away glittery glue from clothes...

wash away paint from paws and nose.

Wash away furious felt tip scribbles...

splats and spots and drips and dribbles.

And stop!

"Poor, brave, dizzy Bear."

"Clean, fluffy, wash-a-bye Bear."

"But now you don't look like Bear...

you don't smell like Bear...

you don't taste like Bear...

and you don't feel like Bear."

"Come on Bear,
I know what
to do."

Back through all our teatime fun,

every smear and every crumb.

Back through noisy garden games,
slippery slides and grassy stains.

Back through making things together, me and you for ever and ever.

And stop!

"Now you're my Bear again."

"But Mummy says now *I'm* all smelly and full of bits
so I need a wash, too."

"Mummy," said Flora after her bath.
"Do you think Bear will still love me
now that *I'm* all washed
and clean?"

"Yes," said Mummy, "and he always will."